681 Beverly Drive
Lake Wales, FL 33853
1-877-676-2285
www.crosampress.com

ISBN 13-978-0-9790337-3-5
ISBN 10-0-9790337-3-X

Printed in the United States of America

The Kingdom of Cydinah

By

Dianne Lininger

The Kingdom of Cydinah

As the son of King Emfred's High Magistrate Jaruth enjoyed a sheltered and pampered existence in his beloved homeland the Kingdom of Cydinah, but his comfortable universe is soon to be overwhelmed and consumed in a fiery maelstrom.

Cydinah's enraged citizens seethe with revolution and hunger for revenge against the small select hierarchy of which Jaruth's family are members. While at the same time bestial hordes of feral warriors are rapidly approaching the borders of the Kingdom.

The boy must confront the unknown and the mystical to overcome strong, deep-rooted fears to survive. In the process Jaruth comes to question and alter his own core values as he faces a new era born of cataclysm.

The Kingdom of Cydinah

Table of Contents

The Kingdom of Cydinah

Jaruth shuddered as the rushing sea winds assailed him. The acrid, salty air filled his nostrils, nauseating his senses. His nervous breaths were labored as he struggled to close the window. The bedroom shutters clanged furiously against the outside wall.

"Rumilla!" he called out in panic, "Rumilla!"

Eyes tightly closed, Jaruth made yet another lunge for the elusive shutters. He pulled them closed with a slam. At that moment the servant, Rumilla entered in alarm.

"I heard your call. From the urgency of your voice I feared you were in peril!" she exclaimed.

Jaruth was chagrined. "I had difficulty closing my shutters," he murmured. "You know how I dread looking upon the sea, especially after nightfall. The dark water almost claimed me once."

"If not for your mother's quick response and swimming skill, it would have," the servant said, as she helped him into his bed-clothes. "But that happened years ago, you should be over this by now."

"The memory's vivid,"Jaruth replied."

Rumilla smiled indulgently. "As I recall, you loved the sea as an infant."

"But that was before."

"Remember, how you enjoyed collecting pretty shells in the surf?"

"That's how it happened," the boy reminded, "Mother was calling as darkness fell."

"And you ignored her!"

"But, I could still feel the shells beneath my feet, even though I could no longer see them. I wanted more."

"So, you could not resist wading out just a little further and straight off that sandbar into the deep water. And you being unable to swim, too!"

Jaruth cringed in horror at the memory. "My lungs filled

rapidly. I feared I would perish in that cold, watery blackness, and hideous creatures would feast upon me. They say there are monsters, relics of a previous eon that are repulsive beyond belief!"

"Did you see any?"

"Rumilla, do you ever wonder about dying?"

"That is not a subject I care to discuss," the servant told him. "Besides, if the sea troubles you to that degree, you shouldn't reside by the edge of Cydinah Bay. But you're growing too old for these childish fears. You must force yourself to overcome them or you'll always be a baby." With that she blew out the candle.

Jaruth watched his beloved servant depart. He listened in darkness as she walked away down the long hall. He thought of Rumilla's words and felt ashamed.

Sleepless hours passed. Cautiously, the boy arose. He approached the window slowly. Trembling, he bent over to peek through a slat in the shutter. The latch suddenly came unfastened, startling him! Jaruth gasped. The dense fog had lifted and the moon was nearly full. The view was serene rather than disturbing. The wind was dying down. Still, the boy shook.

His eyes narrowed as he noticed the delineation of an island far out at sea. But no such isle existed, at least not to Jaruth's knowledge. With a shiver, he pulled the shutters closed and hastened back to bed.

The following morning Rumilla had to shake the boy to awaken him. Downstairs, a breakfast of fresh fruit, bread, and milk were waiting. His parents appeared agitated.

"The Tarkons brought down the Monarchy of Bethedava in one attack, only miles from Cydinah," Mother stated with a tremor in her voice.

"According to refugees, Tarkons are more bestial than human,"

Rumilla said, as she carefully unfolded the boy's napkin. "I've heard that in the fervor of battle, should a Tarkon be left unarmed, they'll slash flesh with their sharp fingernails and rip bones apart with their powerful teeth."

Father cleared his throat noisily to cease Rumilla's discourse.

"Those creatures don't even cook their meat," the servant proceeded, "Mostly it's human organs, I'm told."

Nervously, Jaruth swallowed. "King Emfred's Royal Guard and battalion will protect us, won't they?"

Father avoided eye contact. "Do not despair, Cydinah possesses the most splendid defenses imaginable," he assured.

"At the moment, King Emfred had better take note of his disgruntled subjects," Mother said, "I hear whispers they're close to revolt."

Rumilla's hands trembled as she removed an empty bowl from the table.

"Those burdensome taxes the King has imposed are breaking them," Mother continued.

"That's an exaggeration," Father protested, "Our citizens are more prosperous than believed. They always manage to make their dues. I'll hear no more of this pishposh!"

A long silence ensued until the family began rising from the breakfast table.

"Remember, we're attending the Royal Colosseum this evening," Mother reminded.

"Couldn't I stay home with Rumilla, instead?" Jaruth pleaded, "It's only a silly play, not like the Royal Games last summer. This'll be tedious and I'll be bored."

"Since your father is the King's High Magistrate, it's imperative we appear. Besides, you might enjoy it." Mother smiled.

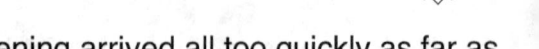

Jaruth was doubtful. The evening arrived all too quickly as far as he was concerned.

The Cydinah Colosseum was filled only with the highest echelons of society loudly chattering away on gossip as well as affairs of state. King Emfred was the last arrival. Everyone stood in deference, until the King was seated. He appeared divinely regal, even omnipotent in his glistening, bejeweled crown and flowing robe.

The image of him imbued Jaruth with pride, and reassured of the might of Cydinah and the devotion of its subjects.

After a nod from His Majesty, the music began and the chorus sang.

"The tale concerns the humorous adventures of a traveling minstrel," Mother whispered.

To Jaruth's surprise, he delighted in all seven acts. In between, the crowd was entertained by jesters and dancing tigers. The boy enjoyed a glorious time. His evening ended all too soon.

"I must tell Rumilla everything about *THE WOOLGATHERING WANDERER*." Jaruth enthused, as they departed the Colosseum. "It was a jolly yarn!" The boy jumped into the coach. He seated himself opposite his parents.

"You'll be whistling and singing those tunes for days." Mother chuckled. "Most assuredly you're too excited for sleep."

"Last night," Jaruth remembered, "I spotted a strange isle, far out at sea. I never realized it existed."

"The fog must have cleared," Mother said. "You might have noticed it before, were you not so fearful of the sea."

"Then it was not my imagination, or a dream!" Jaruth exclaimed. "Why does no one ever speak of it?"

"Because it is cursed, an evil and ominous place," Father drawled.

"Is the isle inhabited?" The boy was eager to know.

Father's expression turned dour. "Only forsaken souls of the damned prowl those shores."

Jaruth's mood changed to a somber one. The subject was abruptly dropped.

Late at night in bed, the boy remained unable to sleep. His curiosity drew him to the window. Jaruth vowed to confront his fear.

The night was clear and cold. A brilliant, full moon gleamed overhead, its luminous glade stretching across the waves and touching the isle.

An obscure human form suddenly appeared ghostlike upon the bright stretch of water. The boy's eyes widened in disbelief. Furtively as a panther, the apparition walked across the moon-glade. Steadily, it moved closer, toward the mainland.

Terrified, Jaruth dashed to his bed, almost stumbling along the way. Beneath the heavy quilts, he trembled.

Though unnerved by the specter, the next morning he told no one, fearing ridicule.

Following breakfast, Mother took the boy aside. "Today, I wish you to accompany Rumilla on a shopping excursion," she informed him. "You shall be her protector."

As a reward for his company, the servant was instructed to purchase for Jaruth a toy, or sweet of his choosing.

"Now stay close to Rumilla at all times," Mother ordered. "There are perils in the village."

As the boy and the servant embarked on their sojourn, the coach suddenly came within view of the palace overlooking Cydinah Bay. The castle was the most breathtaking structure Jaruth had ever beheld. The soaring towers and turrets of marble and gold seemed to pierce the clouds. Surely King Emfred must be the most awesome and powerful person in all creation, he thought.

Hours of encountering vendors passed monotonously slow. The boy grew bored and restless.

"All we've left to purchase is cloth and cheese. Then we may return home," the servant said, "Now, choose a small gift for yourself and be quick."

Jaruth glanced around. "I want to see what's over there." He pointed toward the village's distant, ramshackle interior.

"Nay," Rumilla cautioned, "It's too risky. Stay close!"

Intrigued, Jaruth strained to see beyond. As the servant haggled with a peddler the boy quietly slipped away. Curiously, he began to explore.

The oldest section of Cydinah was the most vast. The further Jaruth ventured, the more ruinous and rancid the scenery became. There existed homeless persons, along with many tattered and abandoned tents. The stench and filth were overwhelming.

Soon Jaruth became desperate to find his way back. To his distress, he discovered himself lost. He took a deep breath. "I must not panic," he whispered to himself.

"Look at the little, genteel boy in the brocade clothes!" someone cackled.

"That one'll make a fine canape for some Tarkon's palate!" another proclaimed.

Jaruth felt a shove from behind. A lad with greasy hair stood with a big smirk.

"Hey! Those shoes with the shiny buckles would fit my ma'ma just fine. She's got tiny feet," he declared.

Jaruth was slammed into a post as a huskier lad emerged, laughing.

"Look at those fancy buttons on his coat. See how they glisten!" he bellowed. "I'll wager we could give those to the tax collector and

the fool'd believe they was gold!"

"Escort me home and you shall be rewarded magnanimously," Jaruth beseeched in desperation. "My father is High Magistrate to King Emfred."

Catcalls and howls of raucous laughter surrounded him. Out of nowhere, a grimy fist walloped him in the face. As his cheek throbbed in pain, Jaruth attempted to rise. He was jerked back into the dirt. The louts were stripping him. Villagers cheered them on, excitedly.

The Kingdom of Cydinah

Chapter II
The Village of Discontent

Jaruth struggled in vain as he felt the dirty hands upon him stripping away his dignity.

"Take everything, the way they do us! Strip him bare, then kill him!" shrieked an old crone, "Take his blood!"

Villagers drew closer to watch, egging them on. "Take his blood! Skin'im and kill'im!" they chanted in chorus. "Skin'im and kill'im!"

"Leave him be!" a solitary, high-pitched voice demanded.

The two louts chortled and sniggered. Avidly, they proceeded with their assault.

"I said leave him be!" the voice persisted.

"Eeeeoow!" the huskier lad yowled.

The other quickly released Jaruth.

There stood a little, flaxen-haired girl attired in rags. She was swinging a heavy stick covered with sharp spikes.

"Begone, both of you!" she ordered.

The louts reviled her mercilessly. The hissing crowd did likewise.

"Get going, tend your business!" the girl hollered. Menacingly, she brandished the stick.

Aversely, the two lads stepped away from Jaruth.

The old crone shook her fist at the girl. "You foul child, I curse you to die!"

As the crowd backed away, Jaruth arose. Modestly, he refastened his torn clothes, now saturated with dirt.

"You shall be rewarded for what you did," he intoned, "Come, I was promised a sweet or toy of my choosing. That choice shall be yours, your due."

The girl sniffed with disdain. She shook her head. "That way." She pointed. "It will lead you out," her voice displayed a sharp edge.

"But I insist you be rewarded. Come, my servant shall give you a few coins at least."

"My actions were not for monetary gain," she snapped. "Your kind reduces everything to that level! I would protect any helpless animal from its tormentors."

"But, I must express my gratitude. Tell me how?"

"You might instruct your father to use his influence with King Emfred to lessen our taxes. Relieved of this burden we might be able to live in a decent manner."

"I don't understand," Jaruth muttered.

The girl rolled her eyes. She began to walk away.

"Wait!" Jaruth cried out, "Don't go, I must know your name?"

"Lisara," she said with hesitation.

Jaruth introduced himself with a gallant bow. "You and I must be the same age." He smiled. "I'm surprised never to have seen you in attendance at the Royal Colosseum. Do your parents not enjoy the games or plays?"

"My folks are long dead from disease," she replied matter-of-factly. "And no one except the wealthy can afford admission to the Royal Colosseum."

"But, how can you survive without parents?"

"Just fine!" she snapped. "I mold vases and decanters from the moss-green clay. I peddle them here. Most of my profit goes toward taxes." She glared at him contemptuously.

"It's true, then. The subjects actually do despise King Emfred. But, I always thought...."

"I doubt you ever thought at all!" she interrupted. "Emfred means to drive the poor from his kingdom by making them poorer. He intends for subjects of status, like you and your family to be the sole possessors of land. Even the successful merchants are not taxed the staggering amount as the poor."

"But, Father says Cydinah's citizens always manage to pay

them, no matter how high."

"Only after extraordinary measures! We can barely afford to feed and clothe ourselves. We've nothing left for luxuries you obviously take for granted!" She nearly spat the words.

Jaruth felt ashamed. "Come back with me and tell my father this."

Lisara shook her head. "I am certain he is aware. It is you who is naive."

"But, you're wrong!"

The girl gave a sigh of disgust. "I shall waste my breath no more." Abruptly, she turned and walked away without a backward glance.

"Wait!" Jaruth pleaded. Sadly, he watched her disappear around a corner.

Rumilla was in a frantic state of tears. She clutched her chest and gasped as the boy took her by surprise.

"Oh my soul! I feared you had been murdered!"

"I nearly was." Jaruth sighed in relief.

"Your parents shall blame me." Her lips quivered.

"But I'm fine, Rumilla. I escaped unharmed."

"Had you not, I might have been strung up by my toes, or flogged till unconscious, or both." She trembled.

Later upon hearing his tale, Jaruth's parents severely rebuked him for leaving the servant's side.

"At least you did not have the temerity to claim a treat," Mother scolded.

"I wanted to give it to Lisara, the girl who rescued me. But she refused," he told them.

"We must conduct a search for this child," Father said. "King Emfred shall present her with a decorated medal. She may wear it proudly."

Jaruth shook his head. "Lisara hates King Emfred, he taxes the poor unfairly, almost to starvation."

His parents recoiled in dismay.

"That is mere silliness, balderdash!" Father shouted. "They are lazy and disloyal. Such subjects are worthless!"

Mother seized the boy's arm. "Should Tarkons attack, they would flee into the mountains to hide, rather than fight beside the King's military and the Royal Guard."

"But, Lisara said...."

"Off to bed with you!" she interrupted. "Let's put an end to this nonsense. You need time to ponder your deed. Shame!"

Darkness was hours away. The long confinement without a meal caused time to drag unmercifully slowly. Disheartened, Jaruth managed to nap awhile. When he awoke, night had fallen. The boy was restless.

He approached the window. The distant shore of the isle was in view. Apprehensively, Jaruth gazed upon the brilliance of the full moon and its golden glade. Eyes narrowed, he searched the waters for signs of the specter hoping it would fail to appear.

Footsteps could be heard coming down the long hall. They paused at his door. A soft knocking ensued.

"Jaruth," whispered Rumilla, "I've brought you something."

He listened to the key turning in the lock. The servant entered carrying a tray with bread, smoked meat, and milk.

"Your parents would be enraged if they knew," she cautioned.

Nervously, Rumilla waited while Jaruth gobbled down the victuals. Afterward, she picked up the tray and quietly departed.

His hunger satiated, the boy decided to return to bed. He walked to the window to pull the shutters closed. As he reached out, his eyes widened. The mysterious apparition had begun its walk across the moon-glade.

Quickly, Jaruth turned away. As he stood quivering, his shame returned. Never would he know peace until his fear was conquered. Sleep would never come to him now. The enigma of the specter must be solved.

"Twice, I have escaped death. I am a survivor," the boy told himself.

Did Rumilla re-lock the bedchamber door, he wondered. Jaruth grabbed the knob and twisted. The door opened.

"The back stairs, I must reach the back stairs," he whispered.

As the boy crept through the long, dimly-lit hall, heavy footfalls came towards him. Jaruth dashed into a small alcove. He hid awkwardly behind a hideous statue of a winged gargoyle.

Mother and Father walked arm-in-arm right past Jaruth.

"Tarkon hordes are poised at our borders, now!" Mother exclaimed.

"Perhaps the remaining monarchies will come to our aide if we be attacked," Father replied.

"Is there one neighboring kingdom that does not hate our Emfred? Should the Tarkons invade, I would be tempted to take our child and find sanctuary in the mountains."

"That is treason. Besides, do not distress yourself, the King shall protect us. I am certain."

"Cydinah may collapse from within, first!"

Jaruth heard the bedroom door slam shut. Stealthily, he crept down the back stairs. He shivered as he stepped outside into the moon-lit darkness. Discovering the gate locked, the boy proceeded to climb over it.

Cold, salty air filled his lungs as he raced down the shore. Jaruth paused to gaze back at his stately home. Icy surf swept over his feet. Startled, he jumped back. The sound of his heart pounded in his ears.

Perspiring and panting, Jaruth searched out a section of thicket to hide and wait. Frigid beads of sweat dripped down his face as he watched the apparition coming nearer.

It seemed to glide across the moon-glade.

"Don't lose courage," he murmured to himself. Jaruth shivered more from fear than cold.

The Kingdom of Cydinah

Chapter III
The Walking Ghost

Trembling, the boy's breathing accelerated. He might be spotted. He must flee. Jaruth attempted to rise, but discovered himself paralyzed with terror. The specter was nearly upon the shore. Jaruth crouched further down to conceal himself beneath the leafy branches.

"Do not look upon the evil apparition," he whispered to himself, "and your safety shall be assured."

However, the boy was unable to control his natural inclination. Curiosity overcame him. Jaruth gasped in astonishment.

Under the brilliance of the full moon a woman of extraordinary beauty, dressed in gleaming silver-white, stepped to shore. Her golden-red tresses were strewn with exotic flowers and precious gems. Many necklaces of silver and gold adorned her. The boy's fear turned to awe and fascination.

Transfixed, Jaruth followed a distance behind. The mysterious woman glided past Emfred's palace and into the village. Jaruth flinched as the ethereal vision entered the squalid and dismal interior. He was hesitant to proceed.

A dark figure lurched from a threshold startling the boy. Roughly, Jaruth was seized by the collar. The moonlight revealed a tall man with a crutch.

"Why'a here?" he demanded, his tone was threatening and he reeked of wine. "What'd you want! You don't belong here, go away!" the cripple demanded.

"But, I came to visit someone, a girl called Lisara," Jaruth lied, his voice was shrill.

"Then do it in daylight, as a decent lad would!" The man released him with a shove. He raised his crutch as if to strike.

Jaruth fled. He ran home without looking back.

Somnolent and exhausted the following morning, the boy had to be vigorously roused from bed by the servant.

"Are you ill?" she inquired with concern.

Sleepily, Jaruth shook his head. "Rumilla, that cursed isle of the damned that no one ever speaks of, someone dwells there."

"Nary a live soul," she replied.

"Are you certain, not ever?"

"Nay, never."

"Ever?" the boy persisted.

"Only if you count that infamous shopkeeper's daughter. But she's long dead now."

"Who?" Jaruth asked curiously.

"Oh, I don't recall her name. It happened ten years ago, you were but a wee infant."

"Well, what happened?"

"She was banished there to die. No one likes to think of it, far less speak of it."

"Why?" the boy wanted to know.

"She was the most beautiful maiden in the kingdom, perhaps the continent. King Emfred personally selected her as his bride. But she refused him, and reviled him publicly to his subjects."

"Why did she do that?"

"The girl was a fool!" Mother snapped. Brusquely, she entered, and loudly began to upbraid the servant.

"It was my fault," Jaruth confessed, "I was curious."

"Rumilla would be wise to watch her words, else she be a subversive influence," Mother fumed.

"But, I want to know," the boy pleaded, "about the lady banished to the isle of the cursed and the damned."

"Indeva was not a lady! She was low-born rabble. You need no further knowledge!" Mother ranted.

"Besides, she's dead and part of the past," the servant added.
Mother grabbed the boy's arm and led him down to breakfast.
Jaruth sat deep in thought throughout the meal.

"You're uncharacteristically quiet this morning," Father noted.

"We could be massacred by Tarkons any day," Mother spoke up.
"I know the child's concerned."

"That's a common anxiety," Father acknowledged. "However, we pray they keep traveling west and bypass Cydinah."

"Should the worst occur, there's always the King's battalion and the Royal Guard," he reminded.

"But are they mighty enough to defeat the Tarkon hordes?" Rumilla asked, as she gathered plates.

Father's coloring became as vivid as King Emfred's robe. "How dare a servant challenge the competency of our King!" He slammed his fist on the table with enough force to cause the remaining dishes to rattle.

"You forget your place. And twice this morning, Rumilla," admonished Mother.

"It was not my intent,"replied the frightened servant.

"Off to the kitchen! Stay out of sight! "Father bellowed.

Mother shook her head with disgust. "Rumilla's tongue has been entirely too loose of late."

"Perhaps she deserves to lose it." Father rasped. "A mute servant is the ideal."

"Nay!" Jaruth protested. "You shan't harm Rumilla!"

"The child is needlessly upset over this triviality," Mother said.
"The Tarkons have us all on edge."

Father placed a hand firmly upon Jaruth's shoulder. "Do not be distressed, son. Our king has again raised taxes, to further arm the realm in the event of attack."

"Do we pay taxes?" Jaruth inquired.

"Certainly not, we are above taxes," Father replied. "Do you think we are common people?"

"But, that doesn't seem fair," the boy reasoned.

"Life was never intended to be fair," Mother told him.

"Shouldn't we do our best to make it such?" Jaruth asked.

"You are talking like a silly child." Father sniffed. "You must begin to think like a man."

"Why should anyone have to pay taxes?" Jaruth wanted to know.

"To support our kingdom," Father expounded, "for example, the Royal Colosseum was built centuries ago with tax funds. Now they're required for maintenance and to provide entertainment. It is necessary! And lest we forget, arms are required to protect us. Cannon powder is a rare commodity in this part of the world."

"Any more inquiries?" Mother asked with exasperation.

"Tonight, there shall be another full moon, correct?" the boy asked.

"I suppose," she replied. "However, you shall be deep asleep."

But peaceful slumber was not his intent. More than ever, Jaruth's curiosity needed to be assuaged. Darkness was awaited with momentous anticipation.

After Rumilla tucked him into bed and departed, the boy quickly re-dressed himself. Vigilantly, he crept down the back stairs and outside into the cold, moon-lit darkness. Nimbly, he began climbing the high gate.

As he neared the top, Jaruth was grappled from behind and thrown onto the damp grass. Father stood over him seething.

"Do you not realize all the horrors that might occur at this unhallowed hour?" he scolded. "What shameful actions were you contemplating?"

"But Father," Jaruth whimpered, "you should be proud, I was

attempting to conquer my fear of the dreaded, dark water by walking the shore."

"Your voice displays stress, it lacks the ring of truth. From now on, your bedchamber shall be locked every night, with Rumilla standing guard outside!"

"Nay!" Jaruth pleaded, "It is unnecessary, please!"

The boy was nearly dragged back to bed, protesting all the way. Disheartened, Jaruth listened to the key twisting in the lock.

Time was quickly fleeing, Jaruth arose. He gazed at the window, his only escape. He bit his lip as he peered over the ledge. He would have to risk a giant leap onto a lower gable. From there, Jaruth could slide onto the balcony. Should the boy fall, he would be seriously injured, if not killed. Jaruth had never a fear of heights before, but now he quaked.

"You can do it," he assured himself. Eyes wide, he took a deep breath and leapt!

A clamorous bang ensued as he hit the gable below and rolled off. Frantically, Jaruth clung to the parapet by his fingers.

Desperately, he longed to cry out and be rescued. He thought of poor Rumilla, who would be punished as well. Jaruth urged himself upward. Mustering every ounce of strength and will-power, the boy foisted himself up and over the top.

Away from his stately home, Jaruth searched out the familiar section of the thicket to hide and wait. Soon, the ghost-like image appeared on the moon-glade.

"Indeva," he whispered, as she stepped ashore. Silently, Jaruth followed. This time, the boy was determined to pursue her all the way. He glanced at his dark clothing. "Better to blend in with the night," he congratulated himself on his cleverness. Never once did Jaruth look back.

As before, the vision glided beyond the palace and deep into the wretched interior of the village. The boy entered with trepidation.

A large congregation of disheveled people emerged from darkness. Some were so gaunt, they appeared to be walking cadavers. They surrounded the mysterious woman, who appeared as luminous among them as the moon itself.

The bitter old crone whom Jaruth recognized from his previous encounter was the first to approach her. "Bless you!" she exclaimed. "You are our salvation!"

"You never fail us," intoned a bony fellow stroking his matted beard, "no matter how often that scurrilous cur raises our taxes!"

With a benevolent smile, the beautiful woman removed the long strands of gold and silver from her neck and passed them out amongst the crowd. She did likewise with the many rings upon her fingers.

"Our eternal gratitude is yours!" cried a frail woman as she balanced a small child upon her hip. "Without you, we would perish!"

The boy stepped closer.

"Seize that woman!" a familiar voice pierced the darkness.

Jaruth turned sharply. There, stood Father with the Royal Guard.

The Kingdom of Cydinah

Chapter IV
The Deep Dungeon

Jaruth watched in dismayed horror as the woman was seized and placed in irons. A burly guardsman stepped arrogantly before her.

"Indeva, this time your death shall be assured." he said with a haughty sniff.

The boy felt his stomach churn.

"Release her!" screamed an indignant voice in the crowd. "Emfred is the criminal, execute him!"

"And his minion, too!" shrieked another.

Increasing in magnitude, the belligerent mob surged forward. Startled, the guardsmen drew their swords. Blades gleamed perniciously in the moonlight. Jaruth was jerked behind his father.

"Try to leave and we'll slaughter you!" hollered a bedraggled man at the forefront. "You're outnumbered! We'll rip off your flesh!"

A soldier seized Indeva's shackles with one hand as he brandished a sword with the other. "A move closer, she dies!"

The mob edged back. Threats turned to vile curses. Caustic grumbling ensued. Slowly, the crowd began dispersing. Indeva was led away in manacles.

Father's strong hands felt oppressive upon Jaruth's shoulders.

"Come son, we must depart this scourged place.

"You followed me," the boy hollered, "you had no right!"

"I am your sire, your protector. Did you believe no one heard that rumpus you created in your foolish haste to sneak away? How rash and perilous an act that was! Never, will you find opportunity again!"

The skin on the back of Jaruth's head started to prickle. He turned around. Lisara stood glaring at him, her face distorted.

Sorrowfully, he attempted to mouth words of regret. But the girl stormed away with a contemptuous toss of her hair. She glanced back only once to make an obscene gesture. The boy felt a rough tug from his father.

"Let us be gone, this place is but an open sewer. Your due awaits! Rumilla, however will be dealt with far more grievously."

"But why, Father? It wasn't her fault!"

"She was placed on guard, Rumilla failed and shall be held accountable."

Upon return, the servant was expelled to the same depth of the King's dungeon as Indeva. Both were sentenced for public execution. Jaruth felt overwhelmed by guilt and self-loathing.

Iron bars were installed on his bedchamber window within hours. The boy was confined to his room for an indefinite period of time.

"I can either make myself ill, or make things right," Jaruth told himself, "But how?" He gazed forlornly at the barred window.

By noon, he heard the key twisting in the lock. Mother stepped inside, she extended her palm.

"Come." She frowned. "Father and I wish to introduce the new servants."

"Servants, more than one?" Jaruth asked in surprise.

Downstairs, Father stood waiting with two girls in their teens. Identical twins, except one had blonde looped braids and the other red. Both were high-cheekboned with pinched faces. There was an aura of unpleasantness about them. The boy grimaced.

"These young women are refugees from the fallen Monarchy of Bethedava," Father said. "The one on the right is Kaema."

The red-haired girl stepped forward.

"And the other is Daema."

The blonde stepped next to her sister.

"You are to accompany our son everywhere, at all times. One on each side," Father instructed. "One more thing," he added. Both servants were handed wooden paddles. "Use these at your discretion, with my blessing."

With a sly smirk, the girls glanced knowingly at each other. Jaruth swallowed nervously.

"Perhaps it was overzealous to sentence poor Rumilla to such a fate," Mother spoke up. "She's been a faithful servant since our nuptials. That malefactor Indeva would never have been discovered, far less captured, if not for the misdeed of our son."

The boy lowered his head. His nausea returned.

"That is irrelevant!" Father snapped. "Her fate has been determined. The issue is closed!"

Jaruth was confined to the main chamber. Kaema and Daema instantly relished their position of authority over their young charge, often striking him without just cause.

"Why are you doing this?" the boy muttered, "Why are you both so nasty to me?"

"Because, you're obviously an incorrigible child." Kaema simpered. "You deserve it."

"And because we enjoy it,"Daema told him. She giggled.

In unison, the girls whacked his backside.

"Stop!" Jaruth cried, "I must leave, it's imperative!"

"Nay " said Daema, "never are you allowed off the grounds again, ever!" She wholloped him over the head with her paddle.

"Never!" added Kaema, striking him harder. "Not even when you're an old man with a hump and a cane."

The two laughed uproariously.

"I want to speak to my mother," Jaruth wailed.

"So the little cry-baby wants his ma'ma," cooed Daema mockingly.

"We'll give you this instead!" Kaema sneered. She raised her paddle high to bash Jaruth.

Her sister did likewise.

"Put those down!" Mother stood in the archway.

Never, had Jaruth seen her so furious.

"Down!" she demanded. "I don't care what instructions my husband has given you, touch my child again and I shall flail you both!"

Jaruth sighed with relief. "Mother, let me go to Rumilla," he pleaded. "I must see her and beg her forgiveness."

She pondered silently for a few seconds. "As well you should," Mother said at last. "Kaema and Daema must accompany you. But do not dare to strike my child," she warned.

Mother issued her written permission. When the three arrived at the dungeon, the twins were refused entry by the Royal Guards.

"Your names are not listed on this document," a guardsman told them, "only the boy's."

Stridently the servants protested, but to no avail. Jaruth was relieved and eager to leave the noxious pair behind.

The sharp, twisting, torchlit steps seemed to burrow endlessly into an odious pit of blackness. Ghastly moaning and wailing greeted the boy and forever haunted him. At the bottom, darkness was so pervasive Jaruth could barely see. Trembling, he proceeded with caution.

"Rumilla?" he called out.

No answer ensued. The boy passed on to the next cell, and the next calling out the servant's name.

"Jaruth, over here! Ahead, to the left!"

"Rumilla?"

Only the servant's outline was distinguishable through the narrow slit in the cell as a dim, solitary torch-light flickered high over head.

"Rumilla, I beg forgiveness of you." Jaruth wept. "Please, forgive me?"

"But I never blamed you, child. This is my fate. I am to die in the best of company, as shall the others here."

"But it's wholly my fault!" Jaruth cried. "If there was a deed I could perform to prevent this, so help me, I would, with all my heart!"

"Boy, come here!" a strange voice beckoned, "over here, boy!" The voice was a woman's.

Sobbing, Jaruth bid his beloved servant a final farewell before treading off to the other cell. When Jaruth peered inside, immediately he recognized the silhouette as that of Indeva.

"Boy, are you as sincere as you sound?" she inquired.

Sniffling, Jaruth nodded.

"Speak up, I must hear you."

"I am trustworthy," Jaruth assured.

Her demeanor revealed skepticism. "Are you willing to succor all subjects of Cydinah, as well as your servant?"

"Anything, any task," he replied in tears.

"I am forced to rely on you." Indeva sighed. "Listen, tonight you must go to the isle off Cydinah and return with riches. You shall walk the moon-glade over the dark water."

The Kingdom of Cydinah

Chapter V
Isle of the Esoteric

Walk the moon-glade, over the dark water. Jaruth gasped at the thought.

"Nay, I can't!" he expostulated. "I don't know how to swim."

"Do not fret," Indeva assured him. "Stride the luminous glade, you shall be safe."

"Please, I cannot."

"You must! It is crucial. Otherwise, the subjects will lose what little they now possess."

"But, I'll travel there by boat in the morning light, huh?" Jaruth asked hopefully.

"Nay, the inhabitants must see you arrive by way of the moon-glade," he was told. "Else, they are unlikely to cooperate and might even do you harm. They must be aware you have been sanctioned by me."

"Jaruth quaked. You mean the cursed and the forsaken damned?"

Indeva reached through the cell and grasped the boy's hand. "The isle is an esoteric one," she explained. "Spirits from another dimension dominate it. Because of a fluke in the cosmos, they must remain in our realm for a millennia."

"I do not follow your words." Jaruth began to blubber in fear and confusion.

Indeva reinforced her grip. "As are most, you're intimidated by that which you're unable to comprehend. Please, do not be startled by what you discover. These entities are not partial to our lot. It took me several difficult years to gain their trust. Remember, your task must be completed. It is essential!"

Jaruth straightened his back with bravado. Inside, he was sick with terror.

"Be quick," Indeva cautioned, "and return the same night. For tomorrow the moon will not be strong enough. You shall likely fall into the sea and drown."

Jaruth felt the blood draining from his face. He began to sweat, his lips quivered. "I am guarded at all times by cruel servants. They await me now. There is no possible way to escape them."

"That way." Indeva pointed. "Around the corner, the grate! Inside, it leads up under the Royal Colosseum and out the performer's entrance."

"But, how do you know?"

"When I was a child," she told him, "my father was imprisoned on a contrived charge. Often, I would visit through that ancient passage, bringing decent victuals for him and the others here. I was never discovered. Go now, be certain to replace the lattice behind you. Hide there, until sundown."

In darkness, Jaruth felt his way around the corner. At the far end, a dim torch burned high above the moldy grate. As he removed the lattice, the metal was so rotted it crumbled onto the stone floor. The boy cursed.

Jaruth had to hurry. He climbed into the empty space behind. Several sections of the passage were so snug that he was forced to hold his breath tightly and stretch painfully in order to squeeze through.

"Indeva must have been nothing but a bony, half-starved wretch," he muttered through clenched teeth, "or else a contortionist."

Covered in cobwebs, he frequently encountered spiders and rats. The boy shrieked as he narrowly escaped the sting of a scorpion. Eventually, Jaruth discovered himself staring into an empty, rectangular room. As he leaned against the lattice it collapsed. Jaruth tumbled hands and elbows first onto a marble floor.

He emitted an agonized howl upon impact. Now, two damaged

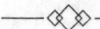

grates would be left behind. Stealthily, the boy slipped out the back entrance.

"The Royal Guard will be searching for me," he whispered to himself. "Must find a secure place to hide." He recalled the tattered, abandoned tents in the village's interior. But would I be safe, Jaruth wondered.

He glanced down at himself. His clothes and skin were badly soiled from the escape. He'd blend in better than ever now.

As Jaruth meandered among the shabby and squalid buildings, a troop of Royal Guardsmen quickly brushed past from out-of-nowhere.

"I dread to stay long in this section after Indeva's capture," one of them told a comrade.

"The little miscreant would stand out here like a bird in a cage of snakes." Another laughed. "Let's search elsewhere."

Jaruth heaved a sigh, but he could never allow himself to feel secure. He spotted a cluster of dilapidated tents ahead. Easily, he found an abandoned one, entered, and closed the flap behind him.

As the hours dragged past, the boy listened to chatter and foot-falls outside, sometimes disturbingly close.

"They're offering a bag o' gold for that lad's return," a booming voice declared.

"You mean the High Magistrate's brat," said another. "That treacherous, little vermin! Why I'd pay a bag o' gold to get him alone, if I had it. He'd be a pile of twitching, oozing, bloody flesh when I was done with the like of him."

"Wonder if they'd give me any gold for just his tongue and eye-balls?" a woman enthused.

Jaruth heard chortles and sniggers.

"That little rat's arse deserves to be delivered in teensy pieces." Someone snorted.

"The more pieces of the lad, the more pieces of gold! That's the way it rightly should be!"

Howls of raucous hoots and laughter ensued. Jaruth clutched his knees in the fetal position. Darkness seemed forever in coming. The boy's stomach growled in hunger. So loud, he was terrified others would hear.

Jaruth peeked out. Daylight still lingered. As he waited, he began feeling that prickling sensation on the back of his head. Nervously, his gaze darted about the tent. The boy screeked! A bulging, blue eye goggled at him through an upper hole.

Instantly, the canvas was ripped apart! A broad-chested man with thick eyebrows and muscular, hairy arms stood over him.

"This is my land and you're a squatter!" he bellowed. "You owe me rent. And I'm getting what's owed, one way or another. You get my meaning, lad?" He licked the blister on his lip.

"That's the High Magistrate's son!" a girl shouted. "the boy who betrayed us!" Lisara stood pointing at him.

Jaruth sprang to his feet as the big man lunged. He dodged past. Others began closing-in. The boy darted through them, racing for his life. He spied the woodlands to the east and sped towards them. The swiftness of his feet, amazed even Jaruth.

Deep in the thick woods, a hodgepodge of strident, cursing voices feverishly pursued him. The boy jumped down the side of a steep knoll and sprinted toward a tree. Hastily, he climbed, concealing himself within its dense branches.

"Where'd the bastard go?" someone shouted.

"Perhaps the ground opened and the devil's claimed his prize," another replied. "He's probably skinny-dipping in those notorious lakes of fire as we speak."

"That would be fitting," said a voice he recognized as Lisara.

"If old scratch ain't got him, then the animals will," a woman asserted. "Lions and bears lurk in these woods, all have a keen craving for human marrow."

"Don't forget the wolves," someone else intoned.

"The lad's finished, that's for certain. Let's go back," another urged.

When night fell, and all was quiet except for the chirping of crickets, Jaruth slithered down. Cautiously, he crept among the dark, dense trees. Sounds were emanating from behind; breathing and foot-falls. Abruptly, the boy stopped.

"It's my imagination," he whispered to himself. Hearing nothing more, he continued on his way.

When he reached the edge of the bay, Jaruth gazed in abject horror upon the black waters before him and the gleaming moon-glade stretching over it. Paralyzed, he was unable to proceed.

"Coward," his voice cracked. "I must," he told himself. "I absolutely must. Nay I can't!" He began to weep in shame.

A branch snapped behind him, then another, followed by hushed voices frighteningly near. Jaruth had no choice. The moon-glade was his only escape. Tightly, he closed his eyes and took a broad step forward. The smell of the salty sea winds brought the dreadful memories surging back.

Certainly, his destiny was to sink into the fathomless blackness beneath the waves. Hideous sea creatures, long thought extinct, and others yet unknown, all abhorrent beyond belief, would feast upon him.

Sweating and trembling, he proceeded. Involuntarily, his eyes suddenly flew open. To his astonishment, the dark, surrounding sea no longer appeared malevolent. The sensation was like gliding upon satin.

"This is wonderment!" Jaruth cried out. The boy laughed heartily at himself.

As he approached the isle, a murky fog began forming. The atmosphere had a strange stench and clammy feel.The boy froze. "Don't lose courage now," he urged himself on.

Fiery breaths singed his spine. Jaruth turned slowly. A monstrous, giant pair of prismatic eyes blazed venomously down upon him.

Shrieking, Jaruth recoiled and cowered. "A sea dragon! A hideous leviathan from primeval times!"

"Exists," hissed an echoing ophidian voice, "legions of us."

Jaruth gazed down through the mist, volumes of horned serpents encompassed him, several were winding around each foot. They began climbing up his legs. The boy flailed, he jumped and jerked violently, screeching!

Through the vapors another giant figure arose before him. It appeared human, until Jaruth noticed glinting green and gold scales patterning the huge, sinewy form. An arm raised and pointed toward the boy. The hand was webbed with extended tentacle fingers.

"GO!" the scaly creature demanded. Its gaze was gelid.

The boy had shivering chills. "Indeva sent me!" he cried out. "Indeva sanctioned me to come."

The creature loomed closer. "Why is SHE not here?"

"Indeva is held prisoner on the mainland. I come in her behalf,"his voice quivered, "I swear!"

The mist began evaporating, and the terrors along with it. The boy's eyes widened in dismay. Before him lay a gloriously eerie land of rolling, mint-green hills awash and gleaming in moonlight. Strange and fragrant wildflowers and trees bearing exotic fruit were everywhere.

"This is an isle of enchantment," he exclaimed as he stepped to shore. Jaruth hungrily plucked a ripe piece of fruit and began enjoying it, laughing as its luscious juice dripped down his chin.

"The melons over here are sweeter," beckoned a parrot with iridescent feathers.

"And the berries are tasty, too, every one," squeaked a small voice.

Jaruth looked down. A silvery, little worm slithered past.

"Actually I came for riches," the boy intoned, "to take back to the mainland as Indeva did. It's for the benefit of Cydinah's subjects."

"Humans are fools," sibilated a voice beyond the rocks,"they deserve whatever befalls them."

"But Indeva is our friend," countered another, "we are obliged to facilitate this child."

Compelled by curiosity, Jaruth peered over the rocks. He blinked in disbelief. Below, were a cluster of tortoises with ornate shells. But their necks were smooth and creamy white displaying the heads and faces of comely women. Some wore silver, gold, or pearl clips in their skillfully styled hair. Jaruth looked closer. Their hands and feet were human as well, with the nails colorfully polished.

"Eeeow!" Jaruth yelped. His ankle began to smart as he jumped back in surprise. One of them had nipped him.

"What are you staring at, nincompoop!" she snapped.

"I was only admiring unique beauty," he told her. "I've seen none finer," Jaruth lied.

"Behave yourself!" another tortoise admonished. "The poor lad is here to aide Indeva."

"I don't believe it," asserted the snapping turtle, "I think he wants those riches for himself."

"We shall help you," said still another. "We dive for sunken treasure, the bounty is endless."

The tortoises huddled and whispered among themselves. After

which, they waddled en masse to the foamy surf and swam out to sea.

"We shan't fail you, lad!" a straggler yelled.

The boy was exuberant. Excitedly, Jaruth began to explore the wonders of the isle, sampling its sweet, exotic delicacy of fruits along the way. Eventually, when his belly became full, he grew sleepy. This was night after all. As one-by-one of the tortoises returned with treasure, the boy found a secluded, mossy spot to nap. Hours passed.

When Jaruth awoke, the incipient rays of dawn were streaming over the horizon far out at sea.

"What am I doing still here!" he cried with alarm as he raced to the shore. It's too late!" the boy wailed, "It's too late!"

For the moon-glade had long since vanished.

The Kingdom of Cydinah

Chapter VI
The Battle for Cydinah

"Why did you fail to awaken me?" Jaruth hollered. He glanced accusingly among the isle's many creatures.

"We thought you had departed," replied a tortoise. "We did think it odd. But you were not seen."

"Never did we imagine you'd fall asleep with so much at stake," exclaimed a parrot indignantly.

Jaruth felt his face burn with shame. "Whatever shall I do now?" he pleaded.

"Swim," said a tortoise, "swim to the mainland."

"But I can't, I don't know how!" the boy cried. "And tonight the moon-glade will not be strong enough to hold me. I shall drown!"

"You've quite a dilemma," squeaked the silvery, little worm.

"Poor boy, poor foolish boy," intoned one of the tortoises. "Poor boy, poor foolish boy!"

Her turtle clan joined in the sentiment along with a chorus of birds. "Poor boy, poor foolish boy!"

The words assailed Jaruth's dignity as well as his ears. Dejectedly, he sat, for hours on the shore, watching the waves and the mainland beyond. The taunting cries resounded in his consciousness. The temptation to throw himself into the sea was strong.

As the sun climbed higher in the morning sky, he noticed an object on the water, floating towards him. As it neared, he could see it was a canoe. Inside, sat a girl paddling frantically, her flaxen hair blowing in the wind.

"Lisara!" In a frenzy, Jaruth waved wildly, jumping up and down. He raced into the surf to greet her. "Lisara, how ever did you know?"

The girl appeared distressed and preoccupied. "Cydinah is under siege," she told him. "Tarkon hordes are invading from the North. The King's battalion and most of the Royal Guard are there. Many are fleeing into the mountains to hide. Everything's chaotic!"

"My parents!" Jaruth cried.

"Those of your ilk are under the King's protection." She sneered. "Indeva remains prisoner. Should the Kingdom fall, her fate shall fare no better among the savages."

"You never explained, why you came," the boy demanded to know.

Lisara hesitated. "I was with two men and a woman, we stalked you through the woodlands. When you reached the edge of the bay, they were about to murder you and toss your body into the dark waves. But, when I saw you upon the moon-glade, I assured them Indeva was behind it. All night, I awaited your return. Why are you here, still?"

Jaruth twitched uncomfortably. He shuffled his feet. "I was detained," he muttered.

"I doubt it shall matter, now." She sighed. "Taxes have been suspended due to the siege. But all prisoners must be rescued before Tarkons arrive!"

"Perhaps we can buy their freedom?" Jaruth suggested. He pointed to the tortoises's bounty of resplendent jewels, gold, and precious gems glistening in the sun.

Her face beamed with hope.

Quickly, they piled the canoe high with treasure. But there was not space for all. Jaruth crammed numerous rings on his fingers. Most were too big and slipped off. Only one remained, a large emerald encircled in pearls that he placed upon his thumb.

As they paddled toward the mainland the boat began sinking under the weight.

"Pitch it overboard!" Jaruth hollered, "else we drown!"

In panic, the two tossed heaps of gold and jewelry into the rippling waves.

"That's enough!" Lisara shouted. "We're not foundering anymore,

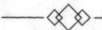

stop!"

After landing ashore, the pair filled their pockets to over-flowing with jewels and precious gems.

"Leave the gold behind in the canoe," Jaruth instructed. "We'll drag it over there and conceal it beneath the shrubbery."

"That's about all we're able to do," Lisara said with a caustic tone to her voice.

The children proceeded to the metropolitan section of Cydinah. The confusion and disorder of which Lisara had related was gone. The once bustling area of commerce was now deserted. And just beyond, the dismal and squalid interior seemed all the more wretched in its abandon.

"Everywhere it's so quiet, and deathly," Jaruth uttered, "like a realm of ghosts."

"The dungeon!" prompted Lisara. "Hurry!"

Only a handful of Royal Guardsmen remained. They adamantly refused to permit the children entry.

"We'll pay lavish riches for the release of all prisoners," Jaruth announced. The boy began emptying his pockets on the ground before them. He nudged Lisara, who did likewise. The guards seemed amused.

"Such garish gewgaws and trinkets," one exclaimed as he examined a sapphire bracelet. "Do you believe us to be fools? These are not genuine!"

"You are fools! Fools and imbeciles!" Lisara retorted. "Emfred's kingdom lies deserted. A wise man would gather up these treasures and flee to safety before the Tarkons arrive."

"And where would two little guttersnipes ever derive such riches?" The guard chortled.

Amid snickers of guardsmen, an officer of high rank appeared.

He seemed agitated. "You are summoned to protect our King!" he ordered.

"But what of our prisoners?" the loquacious one asked.

"Leave them to the Tarkons," came the reply,"our King is of more importance."

The children watched as the men swiftly marched away toward the palace.

"Come." Jaruth motioned. "Follow me!"

He guided Lisara down the steep, twisting, torchlit, steps into the vast dungeon below. The boy's yells echoed throughout the darkness.

"We've come to free you!" he hollered, "every last soul!"

"The key!" Indeva shouted. "Get the key! It hangs in the alcove off the entrance!"

"I'll fetch it," Lisara volunteered. She vanished into the blackness.

Jaruth found his way to the cell of his beloved servant. "Do not fret, Rumilla. Soon, you'll be safe."

After Lisara's return, Rumilla was the first to be released, followed by Indeva and the others.

Lisara grabbed Indeva's wrist. "Come, we'll take you into the mountains to hide."

Gently, the woman pulled away. "Nay, I must remain."

"But, you'll be eaten!" Jaruth expostulated. "The Tarkons are merciless and masters of torture, too!"

"They must be vanquished," Indeva asserted, "every citizen must fight! The King's soldiers and the Royal Guard cannot do it alone."

"But the subjects have all fled into the mountains," Lisara told her.

Indeva noticed the precious gem on Jaruth's thumb. The boy removed the ring and presented it to her.

"Go into the mountains," Indeva instructed the children. "Convince

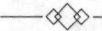

the subjects to return. Not for the King, nor me, but for Cydinah and themselves."

Indeva handed the ring back to Jaruth. "Show this to the people. Inform them I am free and await them. Tarkon hordes must be penetrating Cydinah's borders as we speak, hurry!"

"I know not where in those mountains to search," Jaruth confessed to Lisara as they departed.

"Well I do!" the girl said. "There exists a network of hideouts, mostly caves and tunnels. Our message should travel rapidly through them."

High upon a mountain, Jaruth followed Lisara into an enormous cathedral-like cavern. A large assembly of subjects had made residence there and appeared content in spite of conditions.

"Indeva is free!" Lisara announced. "She implores your return, to fight for Cydinah!"

"When rats sprout butterfly wings and sing like nightingales, we will!" bellowed a man with a pug nose and a filthy beard.

"This is Emfred's fight, not ours!" snarled a stringyhaired woman.

The others all seemed to agree.

"Nay, this is every citizen's conflict!" Jaruth declared. "Fight for your homes!"

"We'll return after the war," said a hag with rotting teeth. "After the barbarians depart, and Emfred is dead."

"Cannot you understand?" Lisara pleaded. "Cydinah will become Tarkon territory. You shall be enslaved, or more likely slaughtered if you attempt a return."

"Then we shall make our homes here, in the numerous mountain caves," stated a ragged-looking youth with thin limbs.

"To live as wild beasts, stranded up here?" Lisara appeared incredulous. "You'd prefer this? You shame me! Indeva came to

your aide in our time of dire desperation, and now you abandon her. The lot of you are nothing but cowards and ingrates."

"And how do we know for certain you were actually sent by Indeva?" inquired a red-haired man with a prominent jaw. "That boy standing beside you is the notorious son of the High Magistrate. This could be a stratagem of Emfred's to trick us into fighting for him."

"I'll prove it," Jaruth declared. He removed the precious ring and passed it amongst the subjects.

"This tells us nothing. It's just a tawdry piece of jewelry," huffed a woman with a crooked nose.

"You're exactly like the Royal Guard!" Lisara exclaimed in disdain.

"Nay," Jaruth shouted, "At least the guardsmen fight to protect their king. These rabble hide like vermin! Indeva is left to the mercy of bloodlusty savages."

"Let us ponder it," said a pale, dark-haired woman with large eyes. "We'll take a poll, then decide."

"There is not time!" Jaruth expounded. "You must return, now!"

"Come," Lisara beckoned to him, "while these spineless poltroons are deciding, we shall be at Indeva's side."

Nimbly, the children headed down the side of the mountain. An explosion of cannon-fire erupted frighteningly near.

"Tarkons are getting closer!" Lisara cried.

"We've failed," Jaruth muttered. "Cydinah will fall at their mercy, as shall we." The boy shuddered. As he fought the urge to weep, Jaruth kept his wits and scurried after Lisara.

The Kingdom of Cydinah

Chapter VII
The Fires of War

Lisara's eyes filled with tears. "At least we shall perish with honor."

Jaruth took a deep, shaky breath. "I pray my parents survive, even if we do not."

"Down there! Indeva and the others are waiting!" she hollered.

"What is that sound, that rumbling?"

"Over in the distance." Lisara pointed. "The Tarkon hordes are advancing."

"But it's coming from behind, they're surrounding us!"

Feverishly, the children hastened down the mountain. Jaruth and Lisara raced to the waiting adults on the edge of the village. The boy bowed his head in anguish.

"There is nary a hope." Jaruth gulped.

"Nay," Indeva replied, "Cydinah's citizens shall seize victory!"

The boy's jaw trembled. "But, you don't understand, the subjects...."

"Over there!" Lisara interrupted.

Jaruth turned to discover a scant handful of individuals trickling down the mountain's side.

"Where are all the others?" Indeva shouted. "The Tarkons are only a hairbreadth away!"

"I think they're coming!" a man hollered back, his voice displayed doubt.

"We need a miraculous strategy to hold our ground with so few!" Indeva exclaimed.

Fire exploded before them as remnants of the King's battalion fled past in terror. Jaruth watched with revulsion as three soldiers fell dead in their retreat. One was severely wounded. In agony, the man attempted to speak.

"Savages have our cannons now." He gasped. His final words, "Cydinah's falling."

Indeva stepped beside the slain soldier. She bent down and

lifted his sword. "We must arm ourselves!" she declared. "Fetch your axes, scythes, pitchforks, tools, and even kitchen utensils; anything which can be used as a weapon."

"Those are useless against cannons!" hollered an old man.

"We have the power to defeat them, but only if we fight!" Indeva urged. "We must hold off the invaders until the others come down from the mountains."

"Suppose they fail to come?" Lisara inquired.

"They shall, the subjects will fight," Indeva assured.

However, Jaruth remained skeptical. But the boy steeled himself for the battle. He glanced about for a weapon.

"See that granite tower." Lisara pointed. "From there, I can see and hear everything. I'm going to hurl rocks at the enemy."

"I'm coming too," Jaruth volunteered.

From atop the tower, they were able to view a breathtaking expanse of the kingdom. Jaruth was transfixed with awe. The spell was broken by Lisara's scream.

"Tarkons! Tarkons in the village!" she cried.

Below, her warning was heeded. The subjects readied themselves for the conflict.

As the enemy hordes encroached, Jaruth was aghast by the sight of them. The Tarkons were a huge race, more bestial than human. Coarse, rat-gray hair largely covered their powerfully-built frames. Long, yellow, and hooked fingernails extended from their huge hands as whetted fangs jutted from their mouths. The women were as ugly and ferocious as the men.

Indeva raised her sword. "Burn the village!" she commanded.

The subjects all fell quiet.

"We cannot, we won't!" a woman spoke at last. "These are the homes for which we fight!"

"Would you have us destroy those?" asked the old man. "Why?"

A disquieting rumble spread amongst the citizens.

"The land will remain, you shall rebuild!" Indeva shouted.

"Rebuild with what? We'll lose everything!" a middle-aged man exclaimed.

"You must trust me. The Tarkons are nearly upon us, burn it!" Indeva ordered.

With hesitation and much reluctance, the subjects followed her command. Jaruth and Lisara watched vigilantly from the tower. Half the Tarkon hordes were only two streets away, now.

"It will never stop them," Lisara muttered, her voice quivered.

"But it may slow them," Jaruth added.

Soon the sky grew black with smoke as fire engulfed most of Cydinah. Its sweltering and flaming, brilliant orange glow permeated the atmosphere.

Frantically, the children hurled rocks from atop the tower. Fire, destruction, and death encompassed them for hours. Dazed and exhausted, Jaruth paused to rest, his clothes drenched in perspiration.

"Don't stop!" Lisara hollered. "The brutes are beating us!"

In abhorrence, the boy watched citizens below dying in battle amidst flames with the enemy. Lisara shoved him roughly.

"Look, through the smoke, others are corning down the mountain!" she exclaimed.

Jaruth resumed his post. The blistering heat was near intolerable.

"Careful, Lisara! Flames are climbing ever higher. They're almost to the top!"

"Don't fret, we're safe!"

A second later, her strident screams blared in the boy's ears. Jaruth swung around. Mere feet away, a Tarkon loomed. Saliva dripped from the voracious fangs. The savage lunged.

Instinctively, the boy flung a rock. The stone left a bloody mark, but the enemy was undeterred. Lisara struck next. A deafening howl ensued. The warrior dropped back. His long, talon-tipped fingers plunged through the air.

In dire desperation, Jaruth and Lisara pummeled with relentless fury forcing the Tarkon further back. A chilling screech, a mingling of wrath and terror resounded as the brute tumbled backward, plummeting into the raging flames below.

Jaruth looked away and wept. He heard Lisara's muffled sobs.

"Are we crying for the Tarkon, or for us?" he murmured.

"Both," Lisara confessed. "Never, have I felt such fear. I'm trembling, still."

Jaruth nodded in concurrence.

"Listen, do you hear that?"

"Something is occurring down in the tower," he whispered. "I'm going for a look." The boy shrieked as he peered down the staircase. "There's more of them! Lots more! They're racing up the steps toward us!"

"That stone bench over there!" Lisara hollered. "Quick, block the entrance!"

Jaruth grabbed the opposite end. However, it was too heavy to raise.

"Push!" Lisara cried. "Push with all your might!"

"They're almost here!" Jaruth screamed. "Forget the bench, grab some rocks!"

Feverishly, in rapid succession the children hurled rocks down the staircase. A thunderous pandemonium arose from below.

"We're beating them back!" Jaruth shouted.

"Only temporarily," Lisara reminded.

"But we've gained some time, let's try the bench again."

Strenuously, they pushed it against the door as a barricade.

Quaking and armed with stones, Jaruth and Lisara waited nervously. With the first assault, the wood cracked and splintered.

Jaruth felt the blood drain from his face as the attacks increased in frequency and force. The door was ready to collapse, while the bench appeared near to crumbling. The boy's breathing accelerated.

"It's ceased," Lisara murmured. "Listen."

"They're waiting for us," Jaruth replied, "night has fallen."

"Cydinah may be lost for all we know," she whispered

"We're nearly out of rocks." Jaruth noticed with alarm. "Use the remainder sparingly."

"I'm so exhausted, I'm nearly ready to die."

"Me too." Jaruth plopped down on the tower floor and stretched out. "I'm going to rest." He sighed.

Wearily, Lisara joined him.

Still trembling, Jaruth closed his eyes. But sleep came quickly.

As dawn broke beyond the mountains, the boy was the first to arise. Jumping to his feet, he peered curiously over the wall. The commotion awoke Lisara.

"There's nothing but smoke and ash all the way to the hills and the sea!" he exclaimed. "Though the palace and dungeon remain."

"Do you see any Tarkons?"

"The smoke's so dreadfully thick, it's difficult to be certain."

Lisara hastened to look for herself.

"Let's go down," she urged.

"Is it secure?"

"We'll take the remainder of the rocks. Fill your pockets."

"We'd better push that bench aside, first," Jaruth told her.

"I'm still in a daze." She wiped the sleep from her face.

"Just imagine had the brutes triumphed."

"Can we be certain they did not!" With a shudder, Lisara reached for the bench.

"Soon, we shall know. Push harder, I feel it moving."

With a mighty shove the bench broke in two. Jaruth's half over-turned and crumbled into pieces.

"At least it protected us at the crucial time," he responded.

The children shoved the debris aside, gathered their rocks and warily crept down the winding, granite stairs.

I can see bottom!" Jaruth shouted. "The tower is empty!"

"Keep your voice down," she cautioned, "they may be waiting outside."

Vigilantly, the pair stepped out amidst the smouldering ruins. A loud hissing of dying embers greeted them.

"I can't see." Jaruth coughed repeatedly as he struggled for breath.

They choked as the heavy smoke filled their lungs. Their eyes stung.

"Head toward the bay," Lisara instructed, her voice was hoarse. "I hear sounds coming from that direction."

"I hear them, too," he said. "I pray my parents are alive and safe."

As they emerged from the smoking rubble, the children happened upon a bedraggled troupe of battle-weary citizens resting beside a muddy pond.

"Did we defeat the Tarkons?" Jaruth was eager to learn.

No reply was forthcoming. The subjects appeared fatigued and traumatized. Lisara hastened to an old woman with pale-blue eyes rimmed in red. The little girl tugged on the woman's fingertips.

"Did we triumph over the Tarkons?" she asked.

Not a sound ensued from her lips, the woman stared vacantly ahead.

"Did we drive the Tarkons away?" Lisara persisted. "I must know!"

The old woman blinked repeatedly, she took a deep breath. Then, a wan smile emerged.

"We have triumphed, Jaruth! Let's rejoice!" Lisara cried.

The rapid hoof-beats of a horse could be heard drawing closer. A sooty-faced rider in charred clothing appeared.

"Indeva awaits to the west," he announced, his voice was high and strained. "She needs every one of you, urgently. Follow me!"

"Haven't we sacrificed enough!" complained a young man displaying his bleeding thigh.

"We have our lives! And our land!" someone shouted. "We must follow!"

Others grumbled. The small troupe decided to follow the horseman, though many reluctantly. Jaruth and Lisara trailed.

Indeva stood amongst a congregation of subjects as pathetic as the ones the children had just encountered. Many were wounded, some appeared in shock, others were weeping.

Indeva raised her sword. "Citizens of Cydinah, we have defeated the Tarkon hordes previously believed to be invincible. Now another challenge awaits us, King Emfred must be dethroned. The Royal Line lasting one thousand years must end this day!"

To Jaruth's alarm, these words ignited and roused a violent passion among the diminished citizens. Their hatred of the King imbued them with a vicious new vitality.

The Kingdom of Cydinah

Chapter VIII
The End of a Millennia

"Fetch the chains! Death to all patricians! Bring forth the blade and the chopping block!" voices thundered throughout the mob.

Indeva raised her sword."Only remnants of the Royal Guard remain. Palace exits have been secured, preventing escape of the nobles and their cohorts."

"Those dastardly frillyfrocks are finished!" shouted a rawboned woman wielding a sword of her own.

"The shameful line of Emfred shall be annihilated!" a man in smoky rags declared. "And its minion, too!"

"Slay them all!" a voice shrieked.

The crowd erupted in boisterous, reverberating cheers as crude weapons were flourished in the air.

Jaruth flinched. He did not share a taste for vengeance against the King and his circle. Uneasy and embarrassed, he said nothing. The subjects swaggered toward the palace.

"Don't forget we have weapons, too," Lisara reminded. She clutched both pockets with pride.

The boy winced.

"Up ahead! The remaining guards!" alerted a feral-eyed woman with a butcher knife at the ready.

Outnumbered, the terrified guardsmen quickly surrendered. Indeva urged restraint as a throng of citizens stormed to the forefront. Shrieking like animals, they invaded the palace, wildly wielding swords, scythes, and axes.

Indeva regained control of the mob outside, keeping them contained. Shouts of vile curses rang from within. Before long, a dismayed man emerged at the entrance dragging a lengthy, curved blade.

"The place's deserted!" he exclaimed.

"No one could have escaped!" insisted a young beggar. "We

covered all exits. It's not possible!"

Indeva ordered the captive guardsmen brought before her.

"Where is your king?" she demanded.

Her words were met with expressions of disdain and stoic silence.

"Mercy shall be given those who lead me to him," she proclaimed, "all others will suffer the royal's fate."

"Emfred did nothing for me!" sputtered a guard with thin lips. "He's in the ulterior chamber!"

The sentry's peers lunged to attack him, but were halted by the mob. Indeva stepped forward, she pointed toward the traitorous one.

"Lead us!" she ordered.

The crowd followed in a steady parade. Many fell silent with awe, for the myriad, grandiose chambers were breathtaking beyond their imagination. The nervous guard led them inside a lavish ballroom. The high ceiling displayed a forest of chandeliers as huge as upturned oaks with crystals the size of pineapples. Covering the west wall was a gigantic tapestry. The scene depicted was a dreamy, ethereal one.

"Here!" The guard pointed. Fingers trembling, be reached behind the left corner.

"Watch out!" squealed Lisara.

Swiftly, Jaruth jumped aside as the heavy wall came sliding towards them.

"There's the hidden chamber!" someone exclaimed.

A cluster of people with startled expressions was revealed.

"Look at those dastards!" yelled a woman with protruding bones. "That's where the nobles and their toadies were hiding, while we fought and died!"

"Pompous filth!" another shrieked.

"See how they cower and quiver now behind their king." A man with a bloody hatchet sneered.

"And look at him." Lisara sniffed with contempt. "This, is our great Emfred? He's just a short man with a paunch and thinning hair. He's common and ordinary!" she responded in disbelief.

Sadly, Jaruth conceded the King appeared rather undistinguished compared to the mighty and majestic deity he had once perceived him to be from a distance.

He began noticing familiar faces among Emfred's many, cowering cohorts. Suddenly, Jaruth spotted his parents. "Mother! Father!" he screamed. Frantically, the boy pushed his way through the mob.

Indeva intercepted him. "Not Yet," she whispered.

"Take them all to the filthy street and stone them! cried a woman shaking her fist with a fervor.

"Nay!" shouted a man raising his scythe, "let us finish them in the chamber. That gaudy rat hole shall become their tomb!"

The vindictive mob clamored and stomped their feet as weapons were brandished. Their crazed eyes revealed a voracious thirst for a bloody revenge. Sick with fear and dread, the boy peered beseechingly into the solemn face of Indeva.

"What is our fate to be?" the King demanded, his voice remained strong.

"Where is the Royal Treasury?" Indeva exacted with equal force.

No answer was forthcoming, only a haughty countenance of disdain. The mob surged forward, blades wielded and flashed amid curses as the nobles gasped and screamed.

"Cease!" Indeva commanded. Sword drawn, she placed herself between the mob and its captives. "Cease!" she ordered.

Grudgingly, the subjects fell quiet. Indeva turned to confront Emfred, the tip of her blade pressed against his heart. "Show me the whereabouts of the Treasury and no one will be butchered."

The King's jaw hardened. Veins appeared on his forehead as he began to perspire. Indeva pressed harder on the sword.

Aversely, he motioned toward a door inside the chamber. Emfred reached under his robe and produced a key. Arrogantly, he flung it across the floor.

"Pick it up!" Indeva demanded. "Unlock the door."

The King hesitated, reluctantly he did as instructed. Loud gasps and sighs were heard. For huge piles of gold, precious gems, and resplendent jewelry of all description were revealed.

"Here," Indeva announced, "are the funds to reconstruct the village, our lives, and rebuild from the ruins of war."

Roaring, resounding cheers and whistles ensued as fists and weapons were thrust and wielded in jubilation. The high walls shook and the chandeliers rattled from the massive commotion.

"Execute the King!" someone shrieked. "And the others too!"

"They have no right to exist!" screamed a woman with grey-streaked hair.

"It's only justice!" yelled a crippled man.

More joined in the sentiment until it became an echoing chorus. Jaruth closed his eyes and trembled, he prayed.

"Nay," Indeva shouted, "I gave my word. But don't imagine for a second they shall go unpunished. In fact, a worse fate should befall them. One more appropriate."

The boy held his breath.

"Emfred, along with his cohorts," Indeva declared, "shall be imprisoned in the village center for the duration of their wretched lives. There to be solely dependent upon the citizens of Cydinah for their daily sustenance. But until our village is restored, they're to be quartered deep within the dungeon depths."

The End of a Millennia

"Our new monarch shall be Indeva," Lisara intoned, "Indeva, Queen of Cydinah!"

Again, the palace quaked from the boisterous display of approval. A bony beggar hobbled over to Emfred and ripped the jeweled crown from his head. With a chivalrous bow, it was presented to Indeva.

"I shall be Monarch of Cydinah for as long as my subjects decree." With aplomb, she gracefully crowned herself queen.

The loud, reverberating clamor of jubilation followed.

"Escort our prisoners to their destiny!" the new Queen commanded.

A toothless man with an eye-patch began prodding the brow-beaten group with a pitchfork toward the dungeon. Jaruth caught Indeva's gaze.

"Wait!" she ordered. The Queen pointed to the boy's frightened parents. "Those two, they're to remain!"

Eagerly, Jaruth rushed to embrace his mother and father. The others were led away.

"I am releasing them in your custody," Indeva told Jaruth. "However, your father shall no longer be High Magistrate. That position shall be filled by a qualified, but more compassionate individual. I suggest your parents learn a trade."

"May we continue to dwell in our grand house by the edge of Cydinah Bay?" Father asked.

"If that is your ancestral home, certainly," they were told.

Jaruth's parents thanked Indeva for their freedom. "Give gratitude to your son, for I am indebted to him," Indeva said. She smiled warmly at the boy before departing to tend matters elsewhere.

"I thought we'd never be together again." Jaruth sighed. He embraced his parents snugly. "I feared you both dead."

"And we of you!" Father replied with relief.

Mother closed her eyes and shuddered. "We imagined all manner of dreadful things," she confessed.

"Whatever became of those twins, Kaema and Daema?" The boy was curious to know.

"Ugh!" Mother exclaimed, "those two horrid girls stole my coach and fled right after you disappeared."

A lanky man with stooped shoulders stepped closer.

"Was your carriage drawn by four cream-colored horses sporting bright, lavender plumes?" he inquired.

Mother nodded.

"I spotted such a vehicle traveling north. It was heading straight into the advancing Tarkons."

"And I saw a Tarkon woman displaying lavender plumage in her hair as she fought in battle," interjected another man. "Those girls probably ended up as the mainstay in Tarkon stew."

Jaruth shivered. "No one deserves such a fate."

"Give praise that the three of us remain unscathed." Father beamed.

The family encircled in a tight clinch. Out of the corner of his eye, Jaruth noticed Lisara backing slowly from sight.

"Wait, don't leave!" the boy shouted as he pulled from his parent's grasp. Jaruth raced into the adjoining chamber.

"Lisara, come back!" he pleaded. "I must acquaint you with my kindred."

"Nay," she replied dejectedly, "they will condescend to me, for my lineage is that of a pauper."

"Lisara, they shall only delight in you. Come back, please." Jaruth was persuasive in his enthusiasm.

Excitedly, he introduced the girl to his mother and father. But to his dismay, their behavior was curt and perfunctory. They were quick to dismiss Lisara. The boy was chagrined.

"Mother, Father, poor Lisara has no one," he expounded.

"That's not true!" the girl snapped. "I have myself and that's a lot!" she straightened her back with pride.

"And you have me," Jaruth replied. "Mother, Father, please, let Lisara become your ward, to be raised as my sister. For she has become such to me already."

Their jolted expressions revealed much, but surprisingly Mother and Father gave in to their son's request.

Lisara however, was reluctant and doubtful.

"Please," Jaruth implored, "we've endured so much together. We've a bond as strong as any blood-kin."

"For you, then," she agreed.

Indeva strode over. She took both children fondly by the hand. "We've altered the course of history," she told them proudly. "We must be accountable as we create the future."

Ensuing weeks were active, often hectic ones. Sounds of hammers, axes, and saws, as well as the clanking of bricks loudly permeated the landscape. Often, Cydinah's new Queen diligently participated in the craftsmanship herself.

Jaruth and Lisara ventured among the clutter and confusion. Falling bricks, lumber, and upright nails were everywhere. The boy spotted Indeva and waved.

"Go back!" she hollered. "You're in the way here!"

"But we want to be part of this!" Jaruth shouted.

"Our village is starting to take form!" exclaimed Lisara.

Carefully watching their steps, Jaruth and Lisara meandered through the reconstruction to Indeva's side.

"Under your reign, Cydinah will become an exemplary kingdom and the years ahead shall be glorious. I can feel it!" the boy enthused.

"A perfect nation is implausible," Indeva patiently told him.

"Many unprecedented problems will arise, but we must confront the challenges."

"You have indeed lead a sheltered existence." Lisara laughed.

Indeva hastily jerked Jaruth to one side. A falling tile narrowly missed him. "It's too hazardous here," she said. She grabbed the children's wrists. "Come, I'm escorting you home in my coach."

Vague, distant sounds of exotic song seemed to dance in rhythm with the breeze, while keeping time with the brisk clip of the horses hoof-beats.

"What is that melody?" Jaruth wondered aloud. "From where does it come?"

Indeva ordered the driver to halt. Intrigued, Jaruth, Lisara, and the Queen stepped from the carriage. The three were drawn to the shore. The afternoon was clear and the isle was visible as they gazed seaward.

Indeva appeared wistful.

"Do you ever miss the island?" Jaruth asked.

"Nay," she replied," it was my sanctuary, rather than my exile. But never my home."

"Look!" Lisara pointed. "Is that a shooting star?"

"I've never seen one so enormous!" Jaruth exclaimed. "Or luminous, see how it blazes in daylight!"

"It hasn't a tail," Indeva noted.

"Its falling on the isle!" shouted Lisara.

A brilliant, blinding flash exploded as the atmosphere became enveloped with incandescence.

Now I see glitter before my eyes," Jaruth cried.

"I too," uttered Lisara.

"It's happened!" Indeva exclaimed with excitement.

As vision slowly returned to normal, Jaruth stared blankly out

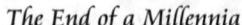

onto the waves. "The isle is gone, disappeared!" he shrieked.

"And nary a vestige remains." Lisara gasped.

The Queen's eyes glistened. "A millennia has ended. The entities have returned to their arcane dimension of origin."

"Thankfully, you're here, not with them," Jaruth reminded.

"It's odd how a sameness continues for years, then abruptly everything's different," said Lisara.

Indeva peered reflectively over the foamy waves. "Often, sweeping changes are the most sudden."

Jaruth agreed.

The End

Dianne Lininger was born in Detroit, Michigan but
raised in South Florida since the age of one. She currently
resides in Vero Beach, Florida.

Dianne has traveled extensively. She has made five trips to Europe,
three to Central America, and has also journeyed
to North Africa, Finland, and Russia.

Dianne's poems have been purchased by READ AMERICA!,
an educational newsletter. She hopes her writings will
empower readers to persevere in their goals.